To Sammy!
Have fun with
Arlie!

Sandra Warren

Arlie
the Alligator

by
Sandra Warren

Music by
Deborah Bel Pfleger

Illustrated by
Deborah Thomas

Arlie Enterprises

HOW TO READ THIS BOOK

The STORY BOOK includes the story, lyrics, sheet music and a word or two about "real" alligators.

Lyrics appear in *Italics,*
Dialogue is in bold type,
Words NOT included on audio tape
appear in small type like this.

When you are reading the STORY BOOK by itself, read ALL of the words; *italics*, **bold** and small type.

When you are listening to the audio tape and following along in the STORY BOOK, read ONLY the words in *italics* and bold type.

"Arlie the Alligator" is available in THREE distinct formats:

STORY BOOK
AUDIO TAPE
ACTIVITY GUIDE: Play book/Song Book/
Reader's Theater Script/Cross-curriculum
Communication Activities and Resources

Library of Congress catalog Card Number: 91-73758

Copyrights:
© WARREN/PFLEGER,1992
© Thomas, 1991 (Illustrations)

First Edition
All Rights Reserved
Printed in the United States of America
ISBN: 1-880175-13-4

Published by:
Arlie Enterprises
SAN 297-4665
P.O. Box 360933
Strongsville, Ohio 44136

Printed by:
Wm. C. Brown Publishing
Dubuque, Iowa

Read Along, Sing Along with...
Arlie the Alligator

Arlie Enterprises   **First Edition**   **All Rights Reserved**

Who is the alligator of a different kind?
Arlie, oh Arlie the alligator.
Who is the one who is so curious to find
Out everything his mind can hold.

Oh Arlie, oh Arlie, is filled with such curiosity.
Oh Arlie, oh Arlie,
Where will your adventures lead?

Who is the alligator always with a smile?
Arlie, oh Arlie the alligator.
Who is the one who's there to crawl the extra mile,
To share a thought with you and me?

Oh Arlie, oh Arlie, is filled with such curiosity.
Oh Arlie, oh Arlie,
Where will your adventures lead?
Where will your adventures lead?
Where will your adventures lead?
Arlie, Arlie.

Arlie slithered onto the beach to enjoy the warm sun. **"Oh no, Arlie, don't go! You'll get in trouble!"** warned his friends.

Arlie paid no attention. He loved new experiences and was very curious about the unusual creatures found at the beach. Besides, he could take care of himself!

He could hear the laughter of the city folk as they played in the sand nearby. Excitement welled up inside him as he carefully peered through the tall grass.

I love the sandy beach, cool water and warm sun.
Hiding behind this reed can be a lot of fun.
Watching creatures big and small;
Laugh and play and run.
How I wish I could be friends with every single one!

Arlie watched for awhile, fascinated by all the different things that he saw. "What strange creatures they are!" exclaimed Arlie. "All different sizes and shapes. Some are tall, some short, some thin as a reed and some rather portly!"

"Alligators aren't like this at all," thought Arlie. "They're either short like me, or growing longer like my big brother and sister, or even <u>looonger</u> like my mom and dad."

Arlie knew that he would lose his beautiful yellow markings when he grew up; all alligators do. But otherwise, he would look just like all the others. You almost had to be another alligator to tell them apart.

He loved to watch the creatures because they did such strange things. The shorter ones were putting sand in round containers and moving them all about. Some were building with them. Others were throwing things, walking in the water and even trying to swim like an alligator!

Some are twirling flat round saucers
High up in the air.
Lots of little ones are digging in the sands... out there!

He even saw some playing alligator! They were lying in the sand, just like Arlie liked to do. "How very interesting," mused Arlie.

I love the sandy beach, cool water and warm sun. I
like to watch the creatures laugh and play and run!

Suddenly a dark shadow fell across Arlie's path, blocking his view. Right before his eyes were the strangest looking objects he had ever seen! Ten round wiggly bumps attached to two towering stalks were staring right into his snout!

"Oh my! Oh my! What could this be?" whispered Arlie under his breath. He was too curious to be frightened.

"**H**ello, Mr. Alligator, what'cha doing?" came a voice from out of nowhere. **Arlie leaned back as far as he could, trying to see where the voice was coming from. His heart was pounding loudly.**

"Oh my goodness! It's one of the little creatures!" exclaimed Arlie. The little creature spoke again. "I said, hello, Mr. Alligator! What are you doing here?"

"**Oh dear me,**" thought Arlie to himself. "**I wish I could understand what it is saying. I am sure it is trying to be friends. What should I do? What shall I do?**"

What shall I do?
I've never been in a situation like this.
What shall I do?
I wish I could get a clue.
Let me think a moment or two.
What would my sister do?
What would my brother do?
What would my best friend do?
There must be some way
To get my message across
Before it's toooo late!
What would my mother do?
What would my father do?
What-would-my-father-do?

WAIT! BY GOSH! BY GOLLY! I'VE GOT IT!
IT'S TRUE.............

Daddy always taught me to bellow!
To bellow! To bellow!
Daddy always taught me to bellow,
"Hey, fellow," he'd say.

One day when you grow up my son,
You will be as large as me.
And you might find that you'll have the urge...
To say a word, or two, or three.

Daddy always taught me to bellow!
To belbw! To belbw!
Daddy always taught me to bellow,
"Hey, fellow," he'd say.

Your great, great, great, Grand-gator,
Was quite the, communicator.
He discovered a way to express what
He felt he had to say.

Daddy always taught me to bellow!
To bellow! To bellow!
Daddy always taught me to bellow!
"Hey, fellow, ... BELLLLLOOOOOOOOOWW!!!!!!"

In a split second he had made his decision. **So, Arlie leaned way back; took a great big...GIGUNDOUS breath, and let out the loudest...**

BELLLLOOOOOOOOOOWWWWW

anyone had ever heard! It was so loud that all the alligators stopped what they were doing. Even the creatures on the beach turned to look.

Arlie's parents moved quickly to his side. "Arlie are you all right?" asked his mother anxiously. At the same time a larger creature swooped up Arlie's new friend and ran in the opposite direction.

Arlie bellowed once more "Wait! Please wait! Oh, I didn't mean to frighten you!" But it was too late. All the creatures were screaming and yelling and running down the beach.

"**Gosh, I didn't mean to scare anyone,**" sighed Arlie. "**We know that,**" comforted his mother. "**Other alligators have tried to communicate with the creatures, but no one has ever gotten through to them.**"

"**You were very brave to try. We are proud of you,**" added his father. "**Time for some fresh seaweed pie,**" exclaimed his mother. "**You've had enough excitement for one day**".

As he paddled off towards home, Arlie looked back one more time. "The creature was trying to be friends, I am sure of it," he whispered.

Right then and there, Arlie made a promise to himself.........

If it's the last thing I do, I will get through
I would like to communicate.
Where there's a will there's a way
And I know it's true
I must find out how to relate.

I understand, I need a plan,
And it might take some time
But I really don't mind.
'Cuz there must be much we can share
If we only knew how.
If we could only break through the barrier,
I'm sure there's lots in common we could talk about.
And I'll make this a challenge to conquer.
I'll make this a challenge to meet.
And as long as I believe in myself and don't give up,
I'll never see defeat.

If it's the last thing I do, I will get through.
I would like to communicate.
Where there's a will, there's a way
And I know it's true
I must find out how to relate!

"**If it's the last thing I do, I will get through to my friend!**" vowed Arlie.

Oh Arlie, Oh Arlie, is filled with such curiosity.
Oh Arlie, Oh Arlie,
Where will your adventures lead?
Where will your adventures lead?
Where-will-your-adventures-lead?
Arlie, Arlie.

The end

ARLIE AND THE "REAL" ALLIGATORS

Arlie is a PRETEND alligator. That means he is not real. He can do anything you want him to do.

He can talk.
He can laugh.
He can dance.
He can think.
He can eat fresh seaweed pie.
And, he can be your friend.

This is Arlie.

REAL alligators aren't like Arlie at all.

Real alligators are very dangerous reptiles.
Do not try to pet them.
Real alligators do not make good pets.
They can not be trained like a cat or dog.
Real alligators do not eat what people eat. They eat small animals, insects, crayfish and other small water creatures.
Real alligators live naturally in the United States and China.
They can be seen in zoos all over the world.

This is a REAL alligator.

To learn more about alligators, go to the library and ask the librarian to help you find books about them.

Arlie
the Alligator
(Sheet Music/Piano)

**Words and Music by
Deborah Bel Pfleger**

© Pfleger, 1984
All rights reserved

Arlie the Alligator

♩ = 104

Words and Music by
DEBORAH BEL PFLEGER

Who is the al-li-ga-tor of a dif-f'rent kind.
Who is the al-li-ga-tor al-ways with a smile.

Ar-lie, oh, Ar-lie, the al-li-ga-tor who is the one who is so cur-i-ous to find out
Ar-lie, oh, Ar-lie, the al-li-ga-tor who is the one who's there to crawl the ex-tra mile to

ev-'ry-thing his mind will hold. Oh, Ar-lie, oh, Ar-lie, is
share a thought with you and me. Oh, Ar-lie, oh, Ar-lie, is

© Copyright 1984 by Deborah Bel Pfleger. All rights reserved.

filled with such cur-i-o-si-ty. Oh, Ar-lie, oh, Ar-lie, where
filled with such cur-i-o-si-ty. Oh, Ar-lie, oh, Ar-lie, where

will your ad-ven-tures lead. lead. Where will your ad-ven-tures
will your ad-ven-tures lead. lead. Where will your ad-ven-tures

lead. Where will your ad - ven - tures lead.
lead. Where will your ad - ven - tures lead.

Ar - lie. Ar - lie.
Ar - lie. Ar - lie.

I Love the Sandy Beach

Words and Music by
DEBORAH BEL PFLEGER

I love the sand - y beach, cool wa - ter and warm sun.

Hid - ing be - hind this reed can be a lot of fun.

Watch - ing crea - tures big and small laugh and play and run.

How I wish I could be friends with ev - 'ry sin - gle one.

NARRATOR: Arlie watched for awhile, fascinated by all the different things that he saw.

ARLIE: What strange creatures they are! All different sizes and shapes. Some are tall, some short, some thin as a reed and some rather portly! Alligators aren't like this at all. They are either short like me, or growing longer like my big brother and sister, or even looonnnger like my Mom and Dad.

© 1984 Deborah Bel Pfleger. All rights reserved.

NARRATOR: Arlie knew that he would lose his beautiful yellow markings when he grew up, all the alligators do. But otherwise, he would look just like all the others. You almost had to be another alligator to tell them apart.

He loved to watch the creatures because they did such strange things. The shorter ones were putting sand in round containers and moving them all about. Some were building with them. Others were throwing things, walking in the water, and even trying to swim…like an alligator!

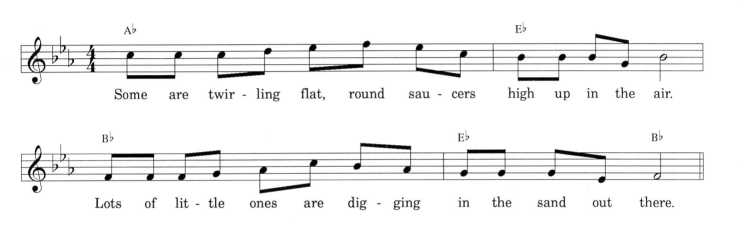

Some are twir - ling flat, round sau - cers high up in the air.

Lots of lit - tle ones are dig - ging in the sand out there.

NARRATOR: He even saw some playing alligator! They were lying in the sand, just like Arlie liked to do.

ARLIE: How very interesting!

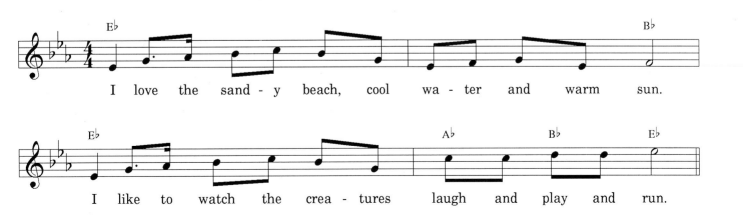

I love the sand - y beach, cool wa - ter and warm sun.

I like to watch the crea - tures laugh and play and run.

What Shall I Do /
Daddy Always Taught Me to Bellow

Words and Music by
DEBORAH BEL PFLEGER

♩ = 108

What shall I do? I've nev-er been in a sit-u-a-tion like this. What shall I do? I wish I could get a clue. Let me think a mo-ment__ or two.

© Copyright 1984 by Deborah Bel Pfleger. All rights reserved.

Dad-dy al-ways taught me to bel-low,————— to bel-low,— to bel-low!—

Dad-dy al-ways taught me to bel-low!————— "Hey, fel-low,"— he'd say,

"One day when you grow— up, my son, you will be— as large as me and you

might find that you'll have the urge——— to say a word or two or three."

Dad-dy al-ways taught me to bel-low,_____ to bel-low,____ to bel-low!____

Dad-dy al - ways taught me to bel-low!_____ "Hey, fel - low,"____ he'd

say, "Your great, great, great grand - ga-tor_____ was

quite the____ com-mu-ni - ca-tor.____ He dis - cov-ered a way to ex-

press what he felt he had to say."

Dad-dy al-ways taught me to bel-low,_____ to bel-low,_____ to

bel-low!_____ Dad-dy al-ways taught me to bel-low,_____ Hey,

fel-low!_____ Bel-low!_____

If It's the Last Thing I Do

Words and Music by
DEBORAH BEL PFLEGER

If it's the last thing I do, I will get through, I would like to com-mu-ni-

cate. Where there's a will there's a way, and I know it's true, I must find out how to re-

late. I un-der-stand, I need a plan, and it might take some time. But I real-ly don't

© Copyright 1984 by Deborah Bel Pfleger. All rights reserved.

mind   'cuz there   must   be   much   we   can   share   if   we   on-ly   knew

how.   If we could on-ly break through the bar-ri-er, I'm   sure there's lots in com-mon we could

talk a-bout. And I'll   make this a chal-lenge to con-quer,—   I'll   make this a chal-lenge to

meet.   And as   long as I be-lieve in my-self and don't give up   I'll   nev-er see de-

feat. If it's the last thing I do, I will get through, I would

like to com - mu - ni - cate. Where there's a will there's a way, and I

know it's true, I must find out how to re -

late.